Hippity Hop and Esther

And Other Stories

Eleanor R DeWoskin

Published by G.L. Design, Boulder, Colorado, USA

Hippity Hop and Esther and Other Stories, 1st Edition

Copyright © 2003 by Eleanor R DeWoskin
Manufactured in the USA
All rights reserved. No part of this book may be reproduced in any form or by any electronic or mechankcal means including information storage and retrieval systems without permission in writing from the publisher, except by a reviewer, who may quote brief passages in a review.

Library of Congress Control Number: 2010913174
ISBN: 1-933983-10-8
ISBN Complete: 978-1-933983-10-3
Cover Art: Eleanor R DeWoskin
Published by G.L. Design, Boulder, Colorado, USA

Table of Contents

Hippity Hop and Esther	5
Little Lucile	25
Eagles	41
Mice, Moths and a Parrot	59
Professor Rodent and Miss Prissy	87
Fred the Anteater	101
Vanilla	117
The Man in the Moon	133
Pinky's Adventure	153
Maurice	167
The Happy Crab	183
Little Mindy	197

Hippity Hop and Esther

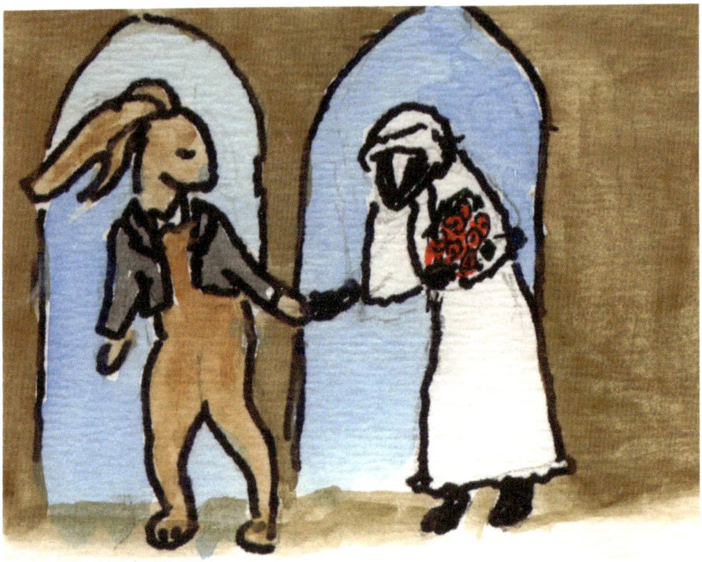

In the Rabbit Kingdom there was a pasture bordered by a hedge. Three bunnies lived happily in these bushes.

There was a mother and father and a little boy bunny called Hippety Hop because he couldn't sit still. It was hippety hop here and hippety hop there all day.

People got so tired watching him that they had to take 'time out' for naps.

Although he was a busy bunny he was also a pretty one and had many admirers. One of them was a little skunk.

Esther was beautiful with her striking black and white stripes but she warned him to "never NEVER startle me."

Hippety's mother wrote a poem for him to remember:

The Skunk

*The skunk
Stunk.
Let us pray
It doesn't
Spray.*

Hippety and Esther got along well and enjoyed playing together. He was careful not to startle her.

Then came the day when the dread disease, Chicken Pox, swept over the land.

Luckily, Hippety was not a chicken so he was spared the most severe form but it was enough to put him in bed for two weeks.

Without him there was no news. Without news life was dull. So dull, in fact, that Father Bunny decided to have an affair and chose little Esther.

Surprise! Surprise! He fell in love with her. Mother Bunny was shocked and hurt when he divorced her for "that little stink pot."

Now Esther's feelings were hurt and she insisted on a proper wedding in the cathedral. Hundreds were invited. Hundreds came.

Esther was extremely nervous but managed to stay calm until the minister said "I know pronounce you man and wife. Let us pray."

She heard it as, "Let us spray." So she did and the odor was so strong at the alter that the good Reverend fainted.

The whole thing was so upsetting that Esther left the room and soon moved to the Artic Circle. There her fur turned pure white and she slept in a seal skin muff that a nice Eskimo made for her.

Hippety Hop didn't think much of his father's choice of Esther and left home. The last we heard he was giving pogo stick lessons to inner city children.

That's all

Little Lucille

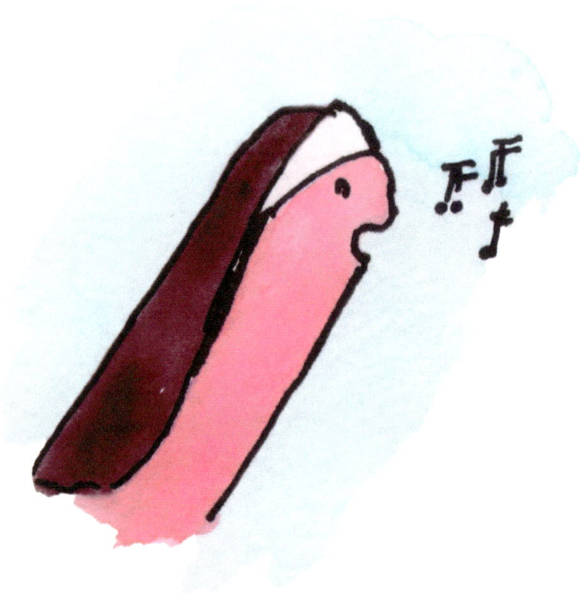

A little worm, Lucille, was an orphan. Early Birds had snatched her parents away. She lived with her aunt.

Lucille's room

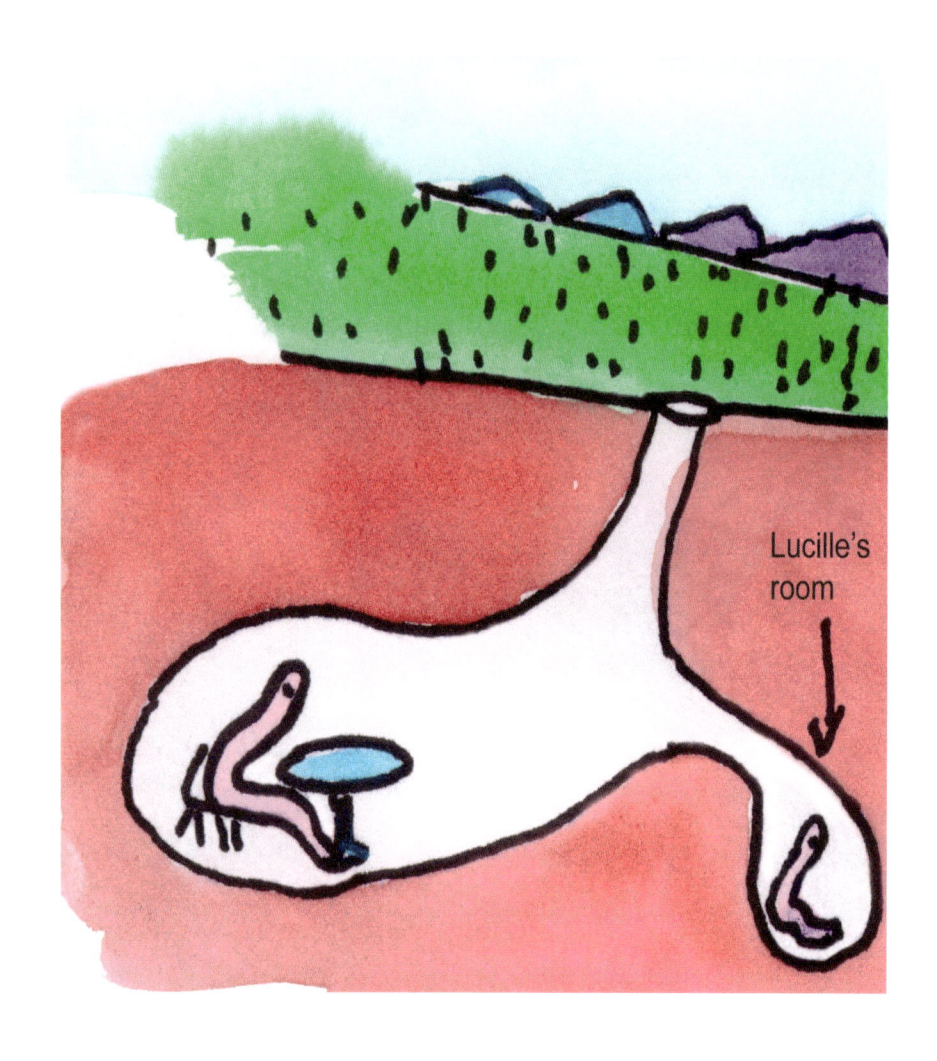

Their home was underground so Lucille was safe as long as she didn't go out. Her aunt warned her about Early Birds. "They get the worms," she said.

"How can I know whether it's an Early Bird?" Lucille asked.

Her aunt wasn't sure, but she thought they had red breasts.

Lucille had one bird friend, Speck Sparrow, that was a vegetarian and lived on seeds. He advised her to avoid all red-breasted birds just to be sure.

That's impossible," she replied. "Cardinals have red breasts. Some finches have reddish breasts. Even blue birds have them. It's confusing."

Lucille decided that she had to hide from all birds, so she disguised herself with a wig, dark glasses and a turtleneck sweater.

No one recognized her except one observant Early Bird that shouted. "That's my worm!"
Her cover was blown.

Lucille took refuge in a convent and donned a nun's habit. She prayed a lot and discovered her voice.

Her voice was so beautiful that the nuns decided to perform "The Sound of Music." The Bishop had to end the applause. He felt afraid that such musical delight might be against the church rules. He told Lucille that she would no longer be allowed to sing.

Lucille was crushed and began to fade. In a few months she was gone.

Everyone grieved. Even the sun had behind a cloud. Then one spring morning a bird song fell from the sky.

The song was so sweet that the earth stood still. The bird book said it was a meadowlark, but all the Earthlings knew it was Lucille's soul on its way to Heaven.

That's All

Eagles
Etc Etc Etc

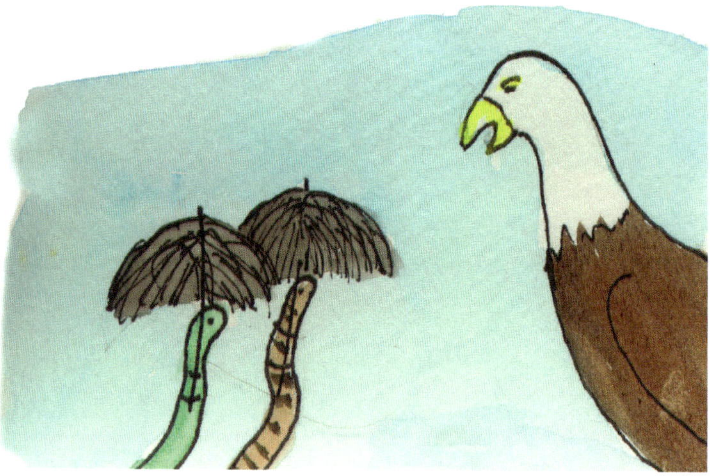

High on a rocky ledge two bald eagles built their nest. They were quite old and were named after a farmer president and his wife, Franklin and Eleanor.

Below them lay a beautiful valley and in it lived a pair of snakes, Howard and Lucy, who were afraid of Eagles. They kept a watchful eye on the sky.

Howard had an inventive mind and devised a kind of harness that held an umbrella. He glued grass to the umbrellas until they looked like little thatched roofs that hid them from the sky.

Howard was proud of himself and, indeed, the eagles were fooled.

"Why in the world are those little thatched houses being moved around?" Eleanor asked Franklin.

"Beats me," he said.

Since she was the curious one, Eleanor flew down to see. She was surprised to find Howard and Lucy under the umbrellas.

"Why the umbrellas?"

"Because there are evil beings in the sky that eat us."

"A monster in the sky?"

"Yes, it flies and it's about your size but all we see is a kind of dark, fluttery thing that snatches us up and away."

Eleanor talked to Franklin. Then both of them flew down.

"It's true that we eat snakes but don't take it personally." Franklin explained, "It's a way of balancing Nature. If we stopped, the earth would be overrun by snakes."

Lucy interrupted "Maybe so, but your balancing nature is no fun for us."

"Let's negotiate" suggested Howard. "We can use crickets as money. "One pint of crickets equals one frog, 2 quarts equal one snake and so on."

This worked until the crickets noticed that a lot of relatives were missing. They rose in protest.

They wrote letters to editors and, on Independence Day, they filled the town square. They carried signs and chirped in rhythm. It was scary.

The snakes didn't dare confront such numbers and Howard thought about a different medium of exchange.

Finally, he thought of mushrooms. Most people like them and they don't complain.

But Howard forgot the fairies. They loved to dance in mushroom rings. They were outraged.

"You are destroying our dance halls" they complained. Howard listened because to displease a fairy is to ask for trouble. Fairies do not like to be crossed.

They are pretty and dainty but short-tempered and willful. Also they like mushrooms to eat.

This objection led to more searching for an acceptable reward.

"I've got it" said Lucy. "Snails!! Snails!!"

"Who eats snails? Yuk!"
"Escargot then."
"Oh, okay. That's different."

So snails became money and snail products rose in price. Howard and Lucy went on an outing and took snail butter sandwiches and red ant wine.

That's All

PS Lunch was delicious and after lunch they made love.

Mice, Moths and a Parrot

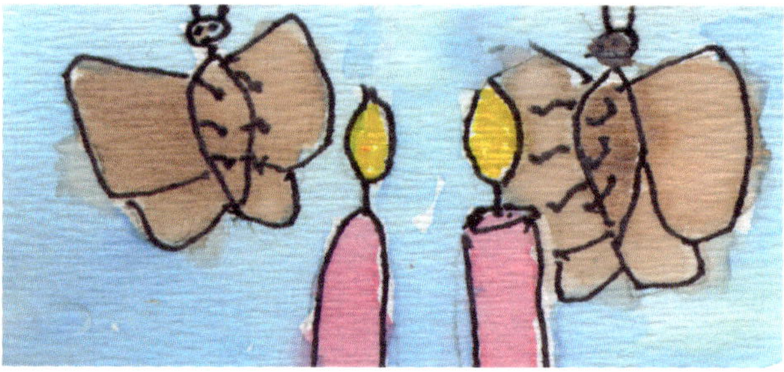

Mr. and Mrs. Mouse were married in a gala event in Betty Simms stable.

They set up housekeeping in Betty's basement. It was cool in summer and warm in winter and she kept her stock of cat and dog food and birdseed there.

There was a pan of water under a slow leek in a water pipe.

In fact, things were so good that Mrs. Mouse ate and slept too much and got fat. She could barely squeeze through the mouse holes.

Mr. Mouse worried. He said "Dear, if the house caught on fire and we had to escape, you would be trapped down here."

"Yes, I know" she answered and ate some sunflower seeds "I worry myself sick about it."

"Myself sick. Myself sick." repeated the old parrot that perched in the basement at night away from cold drafts and summer heat.

"Don't make fun of the victims of obesity" Mr. Mouse said "Obesity! Obesity! squawked Polly.

Mr. Mouse found stacks of old movie magazines and gave them to Mrs. Mouse. They were full of pictures of willowy young ladies.

Mrs. Mouse grew depressed and to despise her plump figure.

"I am a flabby, sloppy mess" she thought and took to using candle light after dark.

When Mr, Mouse objected because it might start the fire he so feared she was strangely resistant. She thought candle light was flattering.

Another worry Mr. Mouse had was that the moths that gathered might singe their wings. They flew so close to the flame.

He spoke to the Queen Moth and she issued an order that moths must stay at least two inches from the flame.

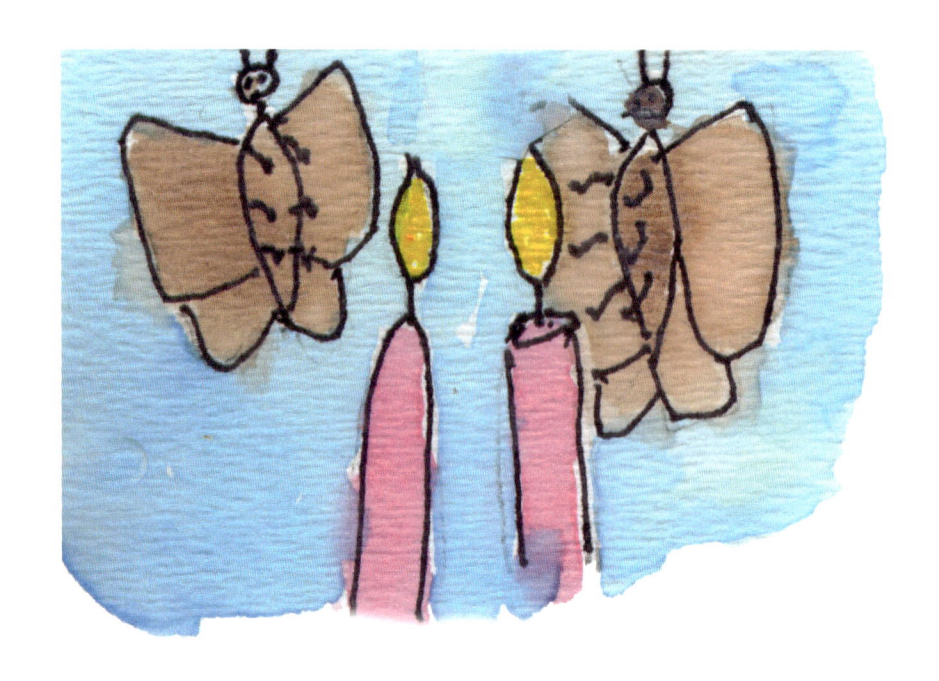

It helped but in chilly weather moths fly close to the candles to warm their feet. They have a tendency to have cold feet and there aren't any socks or slippers small enough for them.

Betty Simms solved the problem by putting out a heating pad set on low for the moths to rest on. In return they promised not to chew holes in her woolens.

In spite of the candle light Mr. Mouse neglected his wife, leaving her vulnerable to other's intentions. When Franklin appeared she would have swooned had she known how. As it was she just stared.

He quickly dismissed Mrs. Mouse with a blithe "You can have her; I don't want her; she's too fat for me." and looked elsewhere.

Now, Mrs. Mouse had sharp hearing and overheard him. She was hurt and when old Polly said "Too fat for me" over and over she knew she had to change.

She joined Weight Watchers but lost so slowly that she asked Polly to keep on making rude comments.

It worked. In a few months she had her girlish figure back and was down to one chin. Polly changed to "good for you, skinny."

Polly began singing Irish love songs of which "Believe Me of All Those Endearing Young Charms" was his favorite.

Meanwhile, Franklin found her more and more charming until Mr. Mouse was ready to challenge him to a duel.

Mrs. Mouse was in 7th heaven. Then one night the house did catch on fire. Franklin escaped first and it was Mr. Mouse who guided his wife to safety.

Deeply touched, Mrs. Mouse arranged for them to reaffirm their love in a solemn ceremony.

That's all

Professor Rodent and Miss Prissy

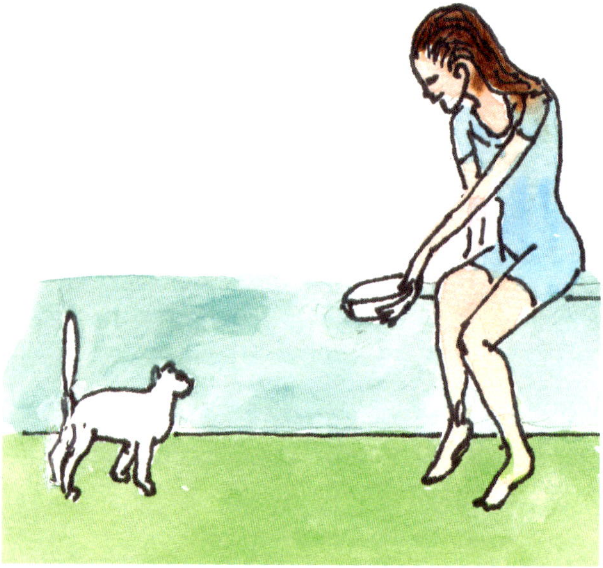

Professor Rodent taught Scatological Studies at Mice College

He did his graduate work at Whiskers University and could 'scat' a cat despite his small size.

He is reported to have declared, "There is no good cat except a dead cat."

But that was in his youth after a nasty back-alley incident, which frightened him.

He has since become friends with old Tom...

...and has participated in FFHC (Food For Homeless Cats) and has made several feline friends.

One homeless lady cat, Miss Prissy, looks for food in garbage cans and dumpsters. She goes to the FFHC shelter too.

Professor Rodent volunteered there and was able to direct her to a household where there was a vacancy. Not even a kitten lived there.

Miss Prissy hung around that house (she called it 'haunting') until the lady there gave in. "You have to wear 'em down," she explained.

Prissy is giving a 'how to' class for homeless cats.

infest = live in
i.e. cats 'live in'
mice 'infest'
people 'abide'
mice, lice and fleas 'infest'
bats, ghosts, mice and squirrels 'infest' attics.
people also 'live in'

The Professor is giving a class in word usage.

This is the way journalists of differing species manage to put "slants" on their reporting without their readers catching on.

That's all

Fred the Anteater

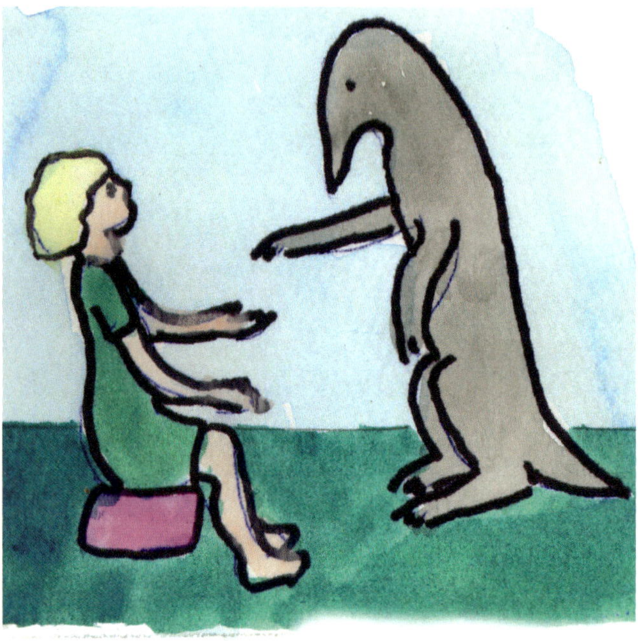

There was a little girl, Betsy, and one morning a large anteater rang her doorbell. Betsy was surprised. She had never seen an anteater before.

He said "Good Morning Miss. I'm Fred and I'm an ant exterminator. Do you have ants bothering you?"

"Yes I do," answered Betsy. "they are coming in under the sliding doors and they're driving me crazy. Ants on the table, in the sugar, ants everywhere.

Fred said "Let me at 'em." He uncoiled his long sticky tongue and licked up the ants. "Mmmmmm good" he said.

Fred had an idea. "Now that the ant problem is solved, let's see what we can do about the bat manure in the attic."

"The what?" Betsy was shocked.
"Where you have bats, you have bat manure. They go together." Fred said.

Fred found a wheelbarrow and shovel and cleaned the attic. Then he fixed it so bats couldn't get in. He spread the manure on the garden where it made the plants grow tall and strong.

Fred suggested that gardeners might buy the stuff but most people didn't like bats or their manure.

Besty spent her time learning to talk to bats that spoke in little squeaks. She tried to talk to the ants but she couldn't hear them.

Betsy's mother baked a big batch of cookies and set them out. The bats loved them and ate most of them. They were messy eaters and left a lot of crumbs.

The crumbs attracted more ants, to Fred's relief, he had lots of ants to eat. He also liked cookie crumbs.

The neighbors planned their yearly picnic and Fred was invited. Betsy's mother said she wasn't going. "Only ants go to picnics."

When she learned that Fred would be there she changed her mind and said "Fred will get rid of the ants. What would I do without him? Spend my summers in a bank vault?"

That's All

Vanilla

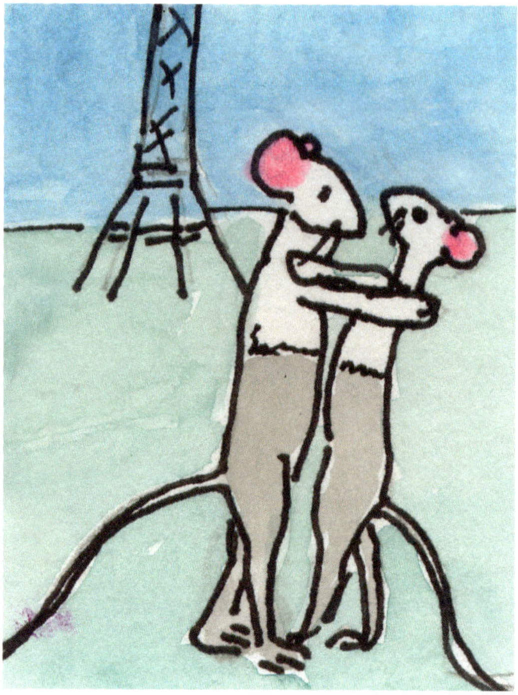

Once upon a time there was a mouse. She was the prettiest mouse in the world and all the boy mice wanted to marry her.

But Vanilla was a gifted artist and was afraid that marriage would hurt her career. She liked to paint flowers.

And portraits

And landscapes

She wrote in her autobiography all about how her beauty had kept people from taking her art seriously.

Finally she decided to become anonymous and hired a friendly panther to pose as the painter of her pictures. She would have peace and quiet.

He was very handsome and was a sensation at the gallery openings. He enjoyed all the attention and compliments he received.

Vanilla was upset and decided to leave this sorry scene and go live in Paris.

She found a nice attic and painted a lot of fine pictures and made many friends.

Edward, a beetle who was a friend of Salvidor Dali, saw her work. He was so impressed that he arranged for a huge party at the opening of her show.

The show was a smash and everybody said she was the cutest thing to come down the pike in years. They made such a fuss over her that she couldn't work. He attic was full of visitors and reporters. She refused all interviews but there was no peace.

Vanilla was in despair.

"I'll insult them and they'll go away," she thought.

She told the reporters that the "public" were all "morons with no more taste than a salamander."

Vanilla didn't know any salamanders so she didn't know what she was talking about.

This angered the salamanders who marched on Washington demanding an apology. The President said he hadn't said any such thing and refused to apologize.

The art critics held a meeting and said they needed to "quantify" how much taste a salamander has.

One of the critics, a giant frog, said their taste was excellent but that most people won't even try one. "They're too cute," he explained.

So the question of a salamander's taste is still unanswered. A raven, that eats them for breakfast, says to leave it that way.

"Who really needs to know?" he asks.

That's All

The Man
In The Moon

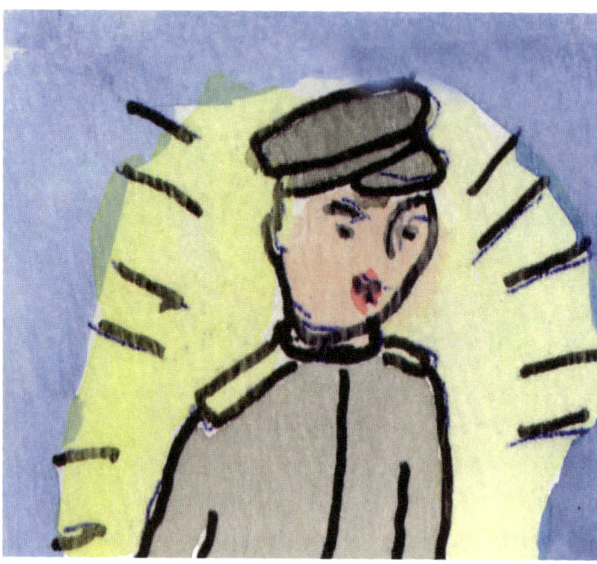

One night the man in the moon, who liked to see what went on on the Earth, decided he was always missing the ends of the stories.

For instance, he saw the police chase a robber into an alley but if the robber ran indoors the moon man never knew how the story ended. Did the cop catch the robber?

Also he saw only the events of the night. The man in the moon longed to live on Earth and he wanted to be a policeman.

There is a powerful fairy whose home is among the stars and the moon man appealed to her.

She agreed to help him and with a tap of her wand on his shoulder he was changed into a policeman —a plain ordinary cop. He named himself George Luna.

This left the moon a blank shining circle which astronomers of Earth were at a loss to explain.

The moon man looked like a human but he was rather plump and he glowed faintly in the dark. He tried to explain it by saying he ate a lot of sunflower seeds.

George might be a policeman but he found that he felt most at home with the 'ladies of the evening' and they made him welcome.

George's friends noticed that he was subdued and slept a lot during the day and became more lively at night. As the full moon approached he became extremely active.

The star fairy began to worry about George. As the month advanced he grew from almost depressed into a storm of activity when the moon was full. Was he out of touch with reality?

Not at all. George read the newspaper where there was often a picture of the 'debutante of the year,' Marjorie Whatsername, daughter of the local jeweler. George had long admired her from afar.

One night while on duty he caught a robber in the jewelry store and arrested him. The owner gave George a big reward and invited him to dinner at his home.

George enjoyed the dinner although he didn't know how to use the knife, fork, and spoon but he watched and soon learned.

After dinner Marjorie and George sat on the porch and watched the sunset but George began to feel that he was supposed to be somewhere else.

The Star Fairy came to see him. She told him, "George your home is the moon." "Oh, so that's it" said George and didn't object when she sent him back.

Ever since George has lived on the moon and when it is full you can see the shadow of his face on that shining circle. George is home.

That's All

Pinky's Adventure

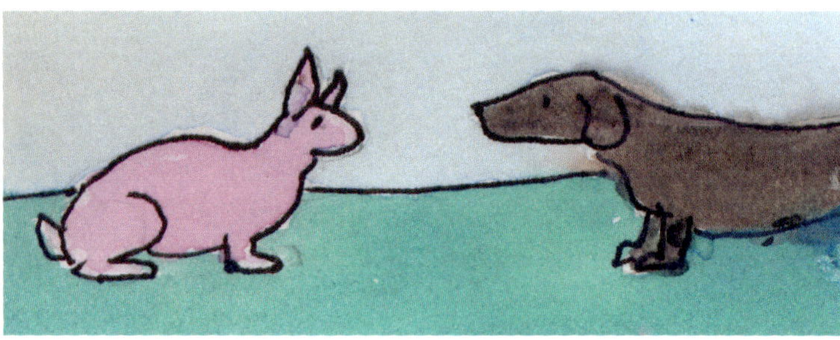

There was a baby rabbit that was born with pink fur and blue eyes. Nobody knew why. His family had brown fur. Had his mother dyed him pink? No. He had been born that color.

His mother gave him a blue collar and tied a blue ribbon around his tail. He and Lucy, a white baby bunny, played together.

Lucy and Pinky played 'house' in a cardboard box. They chewed a door and a window in it.

Pinky's friend, Jane brought them a bag of rabbit food and they invited friends for a feast. With the bunny chow they served carrots and celery sticks. The dessert was sliced apples.

Pinky and Lucy lived peacefully until a large black cat, Satan appeared. He belonged to new neighbors and didn't understand that the rabbits were friends. He chased them. They were afraid of him.

They had an old hole to hide in but Satan made them nervous. They never knew when he would sneak up behind them.

Pinky was a big bunny but Satan was bigger. He ordered the others to 'do this,' 'do that,' or 'don't do this or that' all the time. They wanted to get rid of Satan but how?

Pinky had an idea. "I think we need a dog," he said.

"Good idea" Lucy agreed, "Let's get one."

They went to the Humane Society and talked to the dogs there. The little Chihuhua was the only one that offered to make Satan behave.

"I can lick my weight in wild cats" he boasted.

"That's good," Pinky said. "We want to get rid of a bossy cat. He's huge and black, his name is Satan and he's a control freak.

"Felipe nodded "That's bad. Let me at him."

They adopted Felipe and took him home. When he saw Satan he said "Oh boy! A cat!" and ran toward him. Satan arched his back and hissed.

"What is it?" Felipe asked. "It looks like a cat but it hisses like a snake."

Pinky told him that cats hiss too.

"You don't say" said Felipe and barked at Satan to make him hiss. Finally, they were all so tired they fell into a heap and slept.

That's

all

Maurice

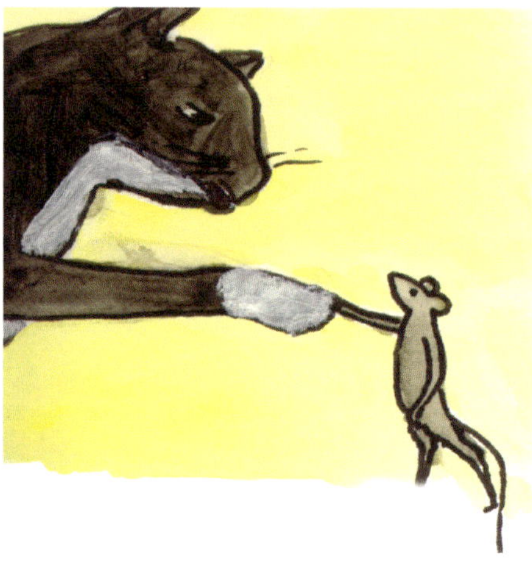

Maurice was a mouse that had the courage of a lion and the tender heart of a loving mother.

He helped rescue a baby bird that fell out of its nest and dug for worms to feed it. He also cared for a baby squirrel.

Imagine how shocked he was to learn that the owner of pitbulls was throwing live rabbits to their pens for food.

What could he do? He called a meeting of the town mice. They were willing to fight but needed help.

Naturally they thought of cats but they can be dangerous to mice. Maurice bravely offered to talk to their leader.

Out of his hole he came and approached Felix, the cat. He carried a white flag of truce.

Felix called out "It's O.K. Come out." So they had a meeting and Felix promised to help fight the dog's owner.

They knew where the rabbits were kept in cages and could free them if they could open the padlocks,

They tried to talk to the president of the SPCA about the rabbits. She couldn't understand.

One evening they gathered around her and pushed and pulled her to follow them to the rabbits. She went.

When they got to the rabbit cages the dog owner was there.

"These are nice rabbits you have" the president said.

"Yes, they don't eat much and they're nice and fat."

"Yes but I can't imagine why you want fat rabbits."

"To feed to the dogs" he explained.

"Oh, I see" she said and decided to set them free. They shouldn't be dog food.

After that the rabbits cats and mice followed Maurice in a protest march past the White House. The President didn't care much but the First Lady nagged him until he signed a bill outlawing the use of living creatures for food.

That's all

The Happy Crab

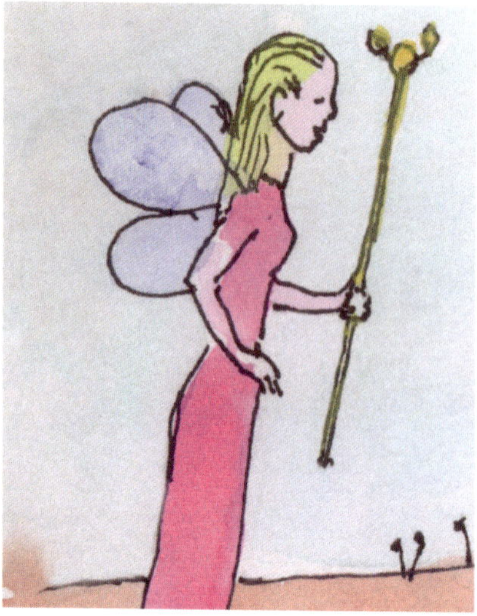

Crabby was a good-natured crab. He laughed and told jokes while his companions complained.

They didn't like this and they didn't like that. Crabby found them depressing. He tried to cheer them up.

He told them about the grasshopper that went into a bar and the bartender said, "Did you know we have a drink named after you?"

The grasshopper thought about this. "Why in the the world would they named a drink 'Bob?'"

But the crabs didn't laugh.

So he asked them, "what did the snail say as he rode on the turtle's back?"

"Whee-ee!"

Then he fell silent.

"Crabby," High Stepper, the heron, said, "you are not your usual jolly self. What's the matter?

"I don't know and I don't care."

"My goodness, you are feeling low."

"You'd feel low too if you lived with a bunch of crabby crabs and had sand in your eyes."

The crab fairy heard him and got her magic wand out of her closet.

"Maybe I can help," she thought. So she flew over to investigate.

"Why are you so cranky and depressed?" she asked them. An old crab spoke up, "for one thing, we live in holes in the beach and get sand in our eyes. Our eyes hurt."

The fairy had an idea. She put their eyes on stalks that held their eyes above the sand.

"You are positively brilliant — a veritable genius," an old crab said. "We can't express our gratitude sufficiently." (The old crab loved big words.)

The fairy just said, "you're welcome," and flew away.

The End

Little Mindie

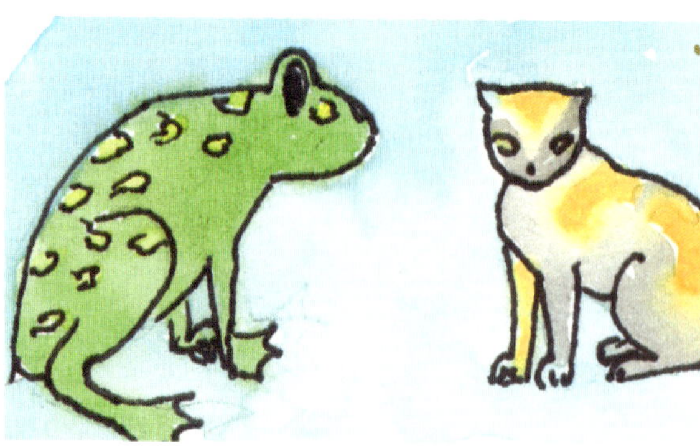

There was a little cat named Mindie that never grew very big. More than that, she had no tail.

Since she was tiny and tailless, she compensated by being especially cute. She was 'cuteness' personified.

She was also very soft and cuddly.

But she felt incomplete. She wanted a tail. She didn't know where to get one. It was discouraging.

She heard about the book, A Tale of Two Cities, and thought it was The Tails of Two Kitties.

Word got around. One day she had a visit from an old frog who said he knew where cattails grew.

This was exciting news and he led Mindie to a pond where, sure enough, there were cattails growing.

A beaver that happened to be passing, cut a tail for her and taped it on her.

She was happy about this until she tried to sit down and found it stiff and uncomfortable to sit on. What a drag!!

Mindie's lady friend, Miss Eleanor, made some tassels for her to wear.

They were made of beautiful colored silks and were very festive. Mindie loved to wear them.

She wore three small ones —one hooked over each ear and one around her neck. She was ravishing!

A tall Siamese gentleman saw her. She reminded him of a Balinese Princess and he fell hopelessly in love.

They moved in together last June. There was talk of a wedding but they have never gotten around to it. Maybe someday.

That's all

Author's Biography

Eleanor DeWoskin, who passed away in 2008 at the age of 93, had become known as one of Boulder, Colorado's local sages. Every day she created her poems, stories and artwork while enjoying a constant stream of visitors who came by to see what she might be working on and to absorb some of her endless good cheer. When asked for advice, she usually replied, "Don't worry about it." Something about the way she said this helped people move on to the bigger pictures in their lives.

Her books contain fragments of Eleanor's natural wisdom captured from different chapters in her own life stretching all the way back to grade school. Eleanor was what her father, a professor of biology, called "range-reared." That means that she didn't have to suffer through the imprinting process called "school" which, some might claim, has a way of ironing out a person's more interesting wrinkles. Eleanor survived intact, complete with her own assortment of lovingly assembled works of art which are her unique commentaries on her journey through life.

By the age of 19, Eleanor had worked her way into the position of writer and editor for a New York magazine called "The Delineator" which eventually was purchased by the publisher of "Ladies Home Journal." The fact that she had spent her childhood running barefoot in the woods did not inhibit her avidly-aquired worldly education.

Eleanor Ritchie DeWoskin was born in 1915 in Williamsburg, VA, as Mary Eleanor Ritchie. She subsequently lived in Flemington, NJ, New York, Florida, Columbia, MO, Washington DC, St. Louis, MO and Boulder, CO.

Correspondence relating to her legacy may be addressed to her son, Cameron Powers
Email: cameron@rmi.net

Other Books
by Eleanor R DeWoskin
Published by G.L. Design
www.gldesignpub.com

Poetic Musings For All Seasons
$16.95
ISBN13: 978-1-933983-04-2

Literally, these Poems For All Seasons, reveal a sensitive and wise personality. There is a poem for everyone somewhere in this 120 page book.

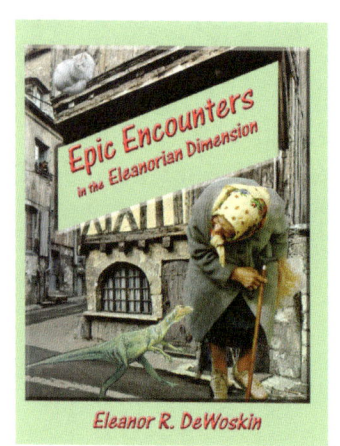

Epic Encounters
in the Eleanorian Dimension
$64.95
ISBN13: 978-1-933983-09-7

Eleanor's improbable and zany but ultimately sane combinations of images are collected in this 130 page book of full color collages.

LaVergne, TN USA
28 November 2010
206523LV00001B